THIS WALKER BOOK BELONGS TO:

_____

_____

_____

First published 2007 by Walker Books Ltd
87 Vauxhall Walk, London SE11 5HJ

This edition including DVD published 2007

4 6 8 10 9 7 5 3

© 2007 Polly Dunbar

The right of Polly Dunbar to be identified as
author/illustrator of this work has been asserted by
her in accordance with the Copyright, Designs and
Patents Act 1988

This book has been typeset in Windsor

Printed in China

British Library Cataloguing in Publication Data:
a catalogue record for this book is available
from the British Library

ISBN 978-1-4063-0834-1

www.walkerbooks.co.uk

Penguin

Polly Dunbar

WALKER BOOKS
AND SUBSIDIARIES
LONDON • BOSTON • SYDNEY • AUCKLAND

Ben ripped open his present.

Inside was a penguin.

"Hello, Penguin!" said Ben.

"What shall we play?" said Ben.

Penguin said nothing.

"Can't you talk?" said Ben.

Penguin said nothing.

Ben tickled Penguin.

Penguin didn't laugh.

Ben pulled his funniest face
for Penguin.

Penguin didn't laugh.

Ben put on a happy hat

and sang a silly song

and did a dizzy dance.

Penguin said nothing.

"Will you talk to me if I stand on
my head?" said Ben.

Penguin didn't say a word.

So Ben prodded Penguin

and blew a raspberry at Penguin.

Penguin said nothing.

Ben made fun of Penguin

and imitated Penguin.

Penguin said nothing.

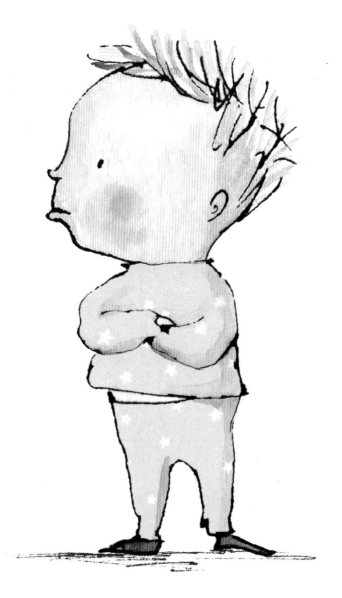

Ben ignored Penguin.

Penguin ignored Ben.

So Ben fired Penguin into outer space ...

Penguin came back to Earth without a word.

Ben tried to feed Penguin
to a passing lion.

Penguin said nothing.

Lion didn't want to eat Penguin.

Ben got upset.

Penguin said nothing.

Lion ate Be

or being too noisy.

Penguin bit Lion
very hard
on the nose.

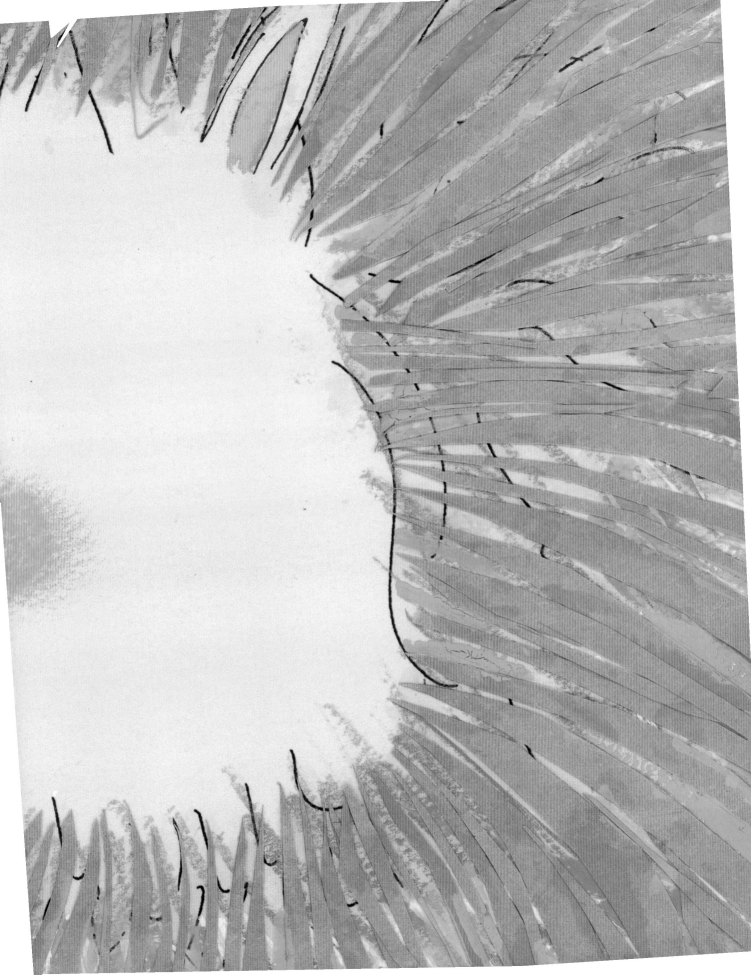

said Lion.

said Ben.

And Penguin said ...

everything!